STINKY STEVENS

Escape from Aunt Smoochie-kiss
Book 4

written and illustrated by **RON WHEELER**

Stinky Stevens: Escape from Aunt Smoochie-Kiss (Book 4)

Copyright c. 2012 by Ron Wheeler
Published by Patchwork
An imprint of Written World Communications
PO Box 26677
Colorado Springs, CO 80936
www.Written-World.com

All Rights Reserved. No part of this publication may be reproduced in any form, stored in a retrieval system, or transmitted in any form by any means—electronic, mechanical, photocopy, recording, or otherwise—without prior written permission of the publisher, except as provided by the United States of America copyright law.

This is a work of fiction. Names, characters, and incidents are products of the author's imagination or are used for fictional purposes. Any mentioned brand names, places, and trademarks remain the property of their respective owners, bear no association with the author or the publisher, and are used for fictional purposes only.

Brought to you by the creative team at www.Written-World.com:
Kristine Pratt, and Corinne Benes

Library of Congress Control Number: 2012939719
International Standard Book Number: 978-0-9829377-7-8

Cover and interior art by Ron Wheeler
Printed in the United States of America

Table of Contents

This book is dedicated to my three kids, Audrey, Byron, and Grace. They are my greatest cheerleaders. This house is awfully quiet ... too quiet, when they're not around. If I could harness their energy I'd never have to pay another electric bill. They keep me young.

Chapter 1: The Alert Is Red

"Red alert! Red alert! Red alert!" screamed Superbear as he raced through the house. He had just seen something that was of great concern to every stuffed animal in the Stevens home.

Careening down the hallway, Superbear rounded the corner into Natalie's room and ran toward her bed where all the stuffed animals were playing cards.

"I said, RED ALERT! RED ALERT! RED ALERT!" he repeated.

"What is it, Superbear?" responded Mr. Bunn, tossing his cards aside.

"Oh come on, you can't quit now," Raggedy complained. "I said, 'Go fish!' I've almost got four of a kind here."

"It's ... it's ..." gasped Superbear, too winded to get the words out.

After several more pants he finally wheezed, "It's a ... red alert!"

"You said that," Raggedy grumbled.

"Take your time," consoled Mr. Bunn. "Catch your breath."

"No time … to catch breath," Superbear continued between gasps. "She's here."

"For crying out loud, who's here?" shouted Raggedy impatiently. "Get on with it."

PANT!
PANT!

"She's here?" asked Mr. Bunn. "You don't mean …"

"Yes, it's her," replied Superbear. "She's back."

"She's back?" Mr. Bunn responded. "It can't be true!"

"It's true! It's true!" lamented Superbear. "She's coming into the house with the others right now."

"She's coming in now?" continued Mr. Bunn.

"Yes, now!" replied Superbear.

"Okay, I've about had it with you two," Raggedy interrupted.

"And so have our readers," she continued. "If you don't start advancing this story pretty soon, they are going to start looking for another book to read."

"It's ... it's ... AUNT SMOOCHIE-KISS!" Superbear blurted out. "She's RETURNED!"

The normally dim-as-a-10-watt-bulb, Horsey, suddenly sprang to life.

"NO! Not Aunt Smoochie-kiss!" he screamed, diving under Natalie's pillow.

Now you know Horsey had to really be afraid at this news, not because he ran and hid, but because he spoke up. Anyone who knows Horsey knows he never says anything, at least not without a lot of prompting. And even then, it was usually preceded with a lot of "ums" and "uhs". That's just the way Horsey was ... but not this time.

While Horsey cowered shivering under the pillow, Raggedy spoke up again.

"Oh … BIG surprise," she deadpanned. "And of course nobody reading this would ever think to look at the cover of this book and come to the same conclusion." She wasn't the least bit caught off guard.

"Stinky Stevens and the Escape from Aunt Smoochie-kiss … there it is, right on the front. It's no big mystery to me Aunt Smoochie-kiss has arrived. Is it to anyone else? I don't think so," Raggedy continued with her insults.

"Okay, I'm new around here," interjected Trixie. "Who is Aunt Munchie-lips, and why should we be afraid?"

"It's not, Aunt Munchie-lips, it's Aunt Smoochie-kiss," Mr. Bunn corrected. "She's Stinky's mom's aunt. Her real name is Aunt Beulah. She's just a little nutty, that's all."

"A little nutty?!?" exclaimed Superbear. He had fully caught his breath by now, and he bravely defended his right to be scared. "Come here and watch her in action."

Chapter 2: Meet Aunt Smoochie-kiss

All the stuffed animals (except for Horsey, who was still cowering under the pillow) crept from Natalie's bedroom into the hallway, and peeked into the living room where all the humans had gathered.

"Come here you children and give your Aunt Beulah some sugar," bellowed Aunt Smoochie-kiss.

"Boy, she's loud," said Trixie.

"That's nothing. Wait until she kisses them," said Super-bear.

SSSMACKK!!!

"Ooo, gross!" said Trixie. "She's practically dripping her saliva all over them. Now I know why you call her Aunt Smoochie-kiss."

"And what's that smell?" she continued.

"That's her perfume," responded Mr. Bunn. "I think she orders it in five gallon tubs from one of those online discount warehouses."

"I don't think her smeller works too good," Superbear added. "That's why she practically lathers up in the stuff. She can't smell it."

"Makes good bug repellant though," Raggedy added. "The flies around here are dropping like ... uh, flies."

"Oh, Steven, bless your heart," Aunt Smoochie-kiss said.

"Oh no, here it comes," whispered Raggedy.

"You poor thing. You're starting to get pimples already … and at such an early age," Aunt Smoochie-kiss continued. "Are you eating too much chocolate?"

"No, ma'am," Stinky replied with a bit of a forced smile.

"What was that all about?" whispered Trixie.

Raggedy responded, "Whenever Aunt Smoochie-kiss says, 'Bless your heart,' watch out! She's about to say something you don't want to hear."

"Huh?" said Trixie.

"I believe it's a long standing tradition among some elderly women from certain parts of the country," said Mr. Bunn. "It allows them to insult others without appearing mean."

"Whoa! That's harsh!" replied Trixie.

"Especially when you consider that some of those certain elderly women are reading this story right now trying to decide whether this book is suitable for their grandkids," Superbear whispered to Raggedy. "I guess you can smoochie-kiss the sales for THIS book goodbye."

"Oooo! Look! There's one," said Mr. Bunn, pointing out at the readers. "Boy, does she look ticked."

"Well, I'm starting to get ticked myself," Raggedy interrupted. "Could we get on with the story please?"

"Oh, and bless your pea-pickin' heart, Natalie," continued Aunt Smoochie-kiss.

"Yikes! She's doing it again," said Superbear. "This time she's added 'pea-pickin'. It's going to be a doozey for sure."

Aunt Smoochi-kiss looked Natalie in the eye and said, "Don't you think it's about time for you to get rid of those stuffed animals in your room?"

"M-my stuffed animals?" replied Natalie.

"Gasp!" cried Raggedy covering her mouth so as not to be too loud. "She's talking about US!"

"See? With Aunt Smoochie-kiss it's always something," Superbear said turning to Trixie. "Last time she came, she was having so many hot flashes, she had all the windows open trying to cool off. I nearly froze my nose off."

"What should we do? Hide?" said Trixie, starting to show some concern.

"In fact," mused Superbear seemingly oblivious to their peril, "After awhile, we were starting to call her 'Aunt Flashie-pants' instead of 'Aunt Smoochie-kiss'."

"Well we'd better come up with a plan in a 'flash' before she starts cleaning house," chimed in Raggedy.

"Wait a second," said Mr. Bunn. "Let's see what happens next."

Mom joined in the conversation with Natalie and Aunt Smoochie-kiss. "Aunt Beulah, I don't think Natalie is quite ready to give up her stuffed animals just yet."

"Yeah! Go Mom!" cheered Superbear as quietly as possible.

"Shhh!" said the others.

"Well, maybe so," responded Aunt Smoochie-kiss. "But I think she's becoming a little too dependent on them. She should be making more friends her own age. I even saw her talking to one of her stuffed animals the last time I was here, bless her heart."

All Natalie could do was hang her head and try to look invisible.

"Can you imagine that?" continued Aunt Smoochie-kiss. "It was like they were really ALIVE."

"I certainly can't," Raggedy whispered. "You guys seem really DULL to me," The others did their best to stifle their snickers.

"Well, did they talk back?" replied Mom to Aunt Smoochie-kiss with a grin.

"Of course not," said Aunt Smoochie-kiss. "Although … it was strange. I could have sworn I saw her little bear shivering."

"See? I told you it was cold," whispered Superbear.

"Well, you did keep it pretty chilly in here. I wouldn't be surprised if all her stuffed animals shivered," Mom said with a smile.

Chapter 3: Crisis Averted … or Is It?

"Okay guys, crisis averted," whispered Raggedy. "For once Aunt Smoochie-kiss is visiting and nothing bad is going to happen. Let's head back to Natalie's room and finish our card game. I'm down three pretzel sticks. I want to win them back."

Aunt Smoochie-kiss continued talking with Mom in the living room. "Well, I can't leave the windows open this time. I've got my grandbabies to think of."

Suddenly, all the stuffed animals froze in their tracks.

"What? What?" asked Trixie. "You guys all look like you've seen a ghost."

"D-did you hear what she said?" asked Superbear.

"She said 'grandbabies', didn't she?" replied Raggedy.

"Quick! To the bedroom! Bolt the door!" Mr. Bunn cried.

The stuffed animals were on the verge of panic.

"Wait! What is the big deal?" asked Trixie.

"The last time Aunt Smoochie-kiss brought her twin grandkids, they were just starting to get mobile," Mr. Bunn tried to explain to Trixie as they were sprinting back to the room.

"Do you know what damage a toddler can do to a stuffed animal?" said Raggedy. "Think of the drool, the chewing, the screams, the grubby little fingers."

When they got to Natalie's room, Mr. Bunn slammed the door shut.

Trixie had had enough though. "Look! I think you guys are WAY overreacting. You need to get a life and stop worrying about little babies."

Superbear helped Mr. Bunn push a chair up against the door to block the way. "These are no ordinary babies. They are named 'Terror' and 'Crazy'," he said.

Just then, Aunt Smoochie-kiss could be heard calling from the living room. "Trevor? Tracy? Where are you?"

"Terror and Crazy, huh?" said Trixie looking at Super-bear as he cowered behind a chair leg. "Look, if you guys want to be scared, that's your business, but as for me, I'm not going to waste any emotional energy worrying about what a couple of harmless babies might do."

"After all, what could they do that would be any worse than what I've gone through. I've lost my arm. I've lived in a gutter. I've been up, and I've been down. How could I be humbled any more than from what I've already experienced?" Trixie exclaimed.

Just then an ear piercing squeal could be heard coming from Natalie's closet.

"WHEEEEE!!!"

"Oh no!" screamed Superbear. "We've locked them in the bedroom with us."

"Quick! Unblock the door!" hollered Mr. Bunn.

"Too late! They see us!" cried Raggedy. "Drop to the floor!"

Chapter 4: Crazy Toddler Terrrorists

Before Trixie had a chance to even turn around to see where the shriek was coming from, a grubby little toddler fist grabbed her around the legs.

"WHEEEEE!!!! A Barfie doll! MY Barfie doll!"

She stripped Trixie's tutu off down to her skivvies and ran around the room screaming,

"WHEEEEE!!! Nakie Barfie doll. Nakie Barfie! Nakie little Barfie!"

She began banging Trixie's head against Natalie's bedpost like a hammer pounding a stubborn nail.

"WHEEEEEE!!!! Barfie! Barfie! Barfie! Barfie!"

WHAM! WHAM! WHAM! WHAM!

"MY Barfie!" Another toddler appeared from the closet to make her claim on Trixie.

"MY Barfie! Mine! Mine! Mine! MINE!"

Like King Kong and a tyrannosaurus rex fighting over Fay Wray, the two toddlers wrestled over ownership of Trixie.

"My Barfie!"

"No, MY Barfie!"

"NOOO! Mine!"

"MINE! MINE! MINE!"

Both toddlers had a deathlike grip on each of Trixie's legs and her remaining arm, and they were pulling all three limbs in opposite directions with all their might. Trixie's friends could do nothing but lay helplessly on the floor.

Outside the room Aunt Smoochie-kiss could be heard calling, "Trevor? Tracy? Where are you?"

Natalie, suspecting something was up, tried to get into her room. "Hey, who blocked the door? Let me in!"

"WHEEEE!!!!"

"Terror" and "Crazy" were having fun even though they were fighting over Trixie.

Suddenly a loud "POP" was heard and Trixie's one remaining arm came flying off.

"OOOO! Broken Barfie! No arm here! An' no arm here! Barfie broken!"

Tracy (although it could have been Trevor … they looked so much alike) then threw Trixie into Natalie's trash can.

For a brief period Trevor enjoyed chewing (or rather, gumming) the remaining Barbie limb for awhile like he was eating a Kentucky fried chicken leg, before he, too, threw his part of Trixie away.

Chapter 5: The Picture of Innocence Is Fuzzy

Outside the door, Natalie was getting persistent. "Trevor and Tracy, you need to unblock the door so I can get in."

Aunt Smoochie-kiss suddenly realized her grandkids were trapped in Natalie's room and she began to panic. "Oh my grandbabies! What have you done, Natalie? They're just innocent little children."

"I didn't do any ..." Before Natalie could finish her sentence Trevor and Tracy had moved the chair and opened the door.

"Gramma! Hold me! Hold me!" they cried, ever looking like the picture of total sweetness and innocence.

"It's okay. Gramma's got you," Aunt Smoochie-kiss said. "You're safe now from that naughty Natalie, playing games with you and locking you in her room, bless her heart."

"But I didn't ..." Natalie tried to defend herself.

Even though the stuffed animals couldn't move, they sure were fuming inside.

"Bless your heart, Natalie," Aunt Smoochie-kiss said again interrupting Natalie.

"Oh, now what?" thought Superbear and the others, "What insult will Aunt Smoochie-kiss throw out now."

"Bless your heart. Your room is so cute. It's a shame you keep it soooo messy with all these filthy stuffed animals all over the place ... bless your pea pickin' heart," said Aunt Smoochie-kiss.

Natalie had to literally bite her tongue to keep from telling her aunt the room was neat and tidy before her rotten grandchildren got into it.

Aunt Smoochie-kiss gave Natalie one of her famous "smoochie" kisses and said, "I need to go change a couple of stinky diapers now. At least I think it's the diapers that stink. Bless your heart, your room stinks so badly I can't tell what it's from. At least I think it stinks in here. I can't tell any more since my snoot's been out of whack. Then I'll be back and look at ways we can rearrange your room to include Trevor and Tracy."

Almost immediately after she left all the stuffed animals were on their feet wanting to know what Aunt Smoochie-kiss meant.

"What did she mean … 'rearrange your room to include Trevor and Tracy'?" demanded Horsey, who was the first to pop up from the safe haven of Natalie's pillow. You knew this was a serious issue to the stuffed animals. This was Horsey's second outburst in one day. Nobody could remember Horsey ever having two outbursts in one year, let alone having two outbursts in one day.

Everyone wanted to know what Aunt Smoochie-kiss's plans were. "Are Terror and Crazy moving into our room?" asked Superbear.

"I-I don't know," replied Natalie, just as stunned as her friends.

Chapter 6: Stinky Breaks Some Stinky News

Just then, Stinky walked into the room with his head down. "I've got some bad news, guys."

Raggedy took one look at Stinky, threw her hands up in the air and said, "Yep! It's true! Terror and Crazy are movin' in."

"They're ALL moving in ... Aunt Smoochie-kiss too," said Stinky. "Mom just told me. Seems that Aunt Smoochie-kiss ... I mean, Aunt Beulah (Stinky couldn't bring himself to call her Aunt Smoochie-kiss ... it just didn't seem funny right now) has fallen on hard times. She has to look after her grandkids, too, and they all need our help."

There was nothing but silence as this news began to sink in.

Almost as an afterthought, Stinky continued, "… and I have to give up my room and sleep on the dining room table."

"What are we going to do?" asked Superbear. "What ARE we going to do?" He was in near panic mode now.

"The first thing we're going to do is get me out of this trash can," hollered Trixie from across the room. "And get me put back together."

"I'm sorry, Trixie," Natalie said. She popped her arm back on and got her back into her tutu. "With all the hubbub going on, I completely forgot about you."

"That's okay," replied Trixie. "I'm sort of getting used to being humbled lately."

"But what are we going to do?" asked Superbear again. "At least with Trixie, you can pop her arm back on. With the rest of us, you rip off an arm and all our stuffin' comes out."

"Hey, getting an arm ripped off isn't exactly a walk in the park for me either," Trixie shot back.

"Come on, gang. Let's not start fighting," Mr. Bunn chimed in. "That won't solve anything."

"I've got news for you, Hare Brain," said Raggedy. "Not fighting isn't going to solve anything either. We're sunk!"

Chapter 7: Always Trust Your Cartoonist

After much thought, Stinky spoke up again. "Guys, guys, … haven't we learned anything from all we've been through in these books?"

Everyone stared at him blankly.

"We've GOT to trust the cartoonist," Stinky implored. "He's the one writing this story. He knows what's best. He cares for us."

"Sure. I feel very loved by the cartoonist right now. Don't you, Superbear?" said Trixie.

All Superbear could do was stare off into the distance and say, "I don't want to have my arm ripped off. What are we going to do?"

Raggedy couldn't resist the unending theological challenge of the moment. "Okay, trust the cartoonist, huh? Who's to say the cartoonist is in charge of all this? Does that mean the cartoonist is to blame for Trixie's abuse?"

"Or did the cartoonist create Terror and Crazy with a free will to do these things to Trixie? And who knows what kind of trouble Aunt Smoochie-kiss has had in her past that has contributed to the way she is, or the way her grandkids are?"

"And who says the cartoonist really cares for us? Did all this happen truly for OUR benefit?" Raggedy was on a roll. "Or did it happen for the cartoonist's benefit? Does his desire come first, since he is the one who is writing and drawing it all?"

Everyone was staring blankly at Raggedy, just as they stared blankly at Stinky earlier. So she continued, "Or … or, maybe it's this … all that has happened to us isn't for our benefit at all, or for the cartoonist's benefit … but it's for the readers' benefit this all has happened. The cartoonist is writing for the readers."

"Yeah, I'll bet that's it. So the readers out there are ultimately to blame for all our problems," Raggedy concluded. "… especially those elderly ones who say 'bless your heart' all the time."

Raggedy then looked toward the others and said, "Well bless your heart, Mr. Bunn. What do you think of this theory?"

Mr. Bunn just sat for a minute with his head in his hands. Then he looked at Raggedy and said …

"Awww, SHUT UP!"

"Why do you always think about this stuff right when we're in the middle of a crisis?" he continued. "Stinky's right. We just need to trust the cartoonist. Who cares why or how it all happens, right Stinky?"

Stinky said, "That's what I said ... trust the cartoonist. That's what Superbear always tells me. Right, Superbear?"

"I said ... right, Superbear?" Stinky repeated looking around for Superbear.

Chapter 8: Superbear Goes Off the Deep End

"Superbear?" he called out.

Superbear was in a different world. "The readers! There's the readers! The readers are in charge. The readers will save me."

Superbear climbed to the edge of the page and stared out into the audience. "Help me, readers. You're the only ones who can save me. Save me from Terror and Crazy."

"Superbear, where are you going?" Natalie shouted. "You can't leave the book. You've got to trust the cartoonist."

"I must grab the bottom edge of the book and pull myself out ... I don't want my arm ripped off," Superbear mumbled as he began to reach outside the book. Of course no drawing can occur off the page so his arm disappeared as he began to reach beyond the bottom edge of the paper.

Fortunately Natalie pulled him back just in the nick of time. One more second and he would have disappeared altogether.

"You're not thinking straight, Superbear," she said.

"You're not thinking, period," added Stinky as he gave Natalie a hand.

"I say you're not thinking, exclamation point," chimed in Raggedy from a safe distance.

"Let me go," Superbear replied. "I'm no good to anyone here. My faith is shot. I'll just bring everyone down. You should have let me fall off the page."

"Oh no, Superbear! Look! Your arm!" Stinky said.

Chapter 9: Superbear Is Un-armed

"What arm?" Superbear replied.

"That's it exactly," exclaimed Stinky. "Your arm is GONE!"

"It must have somehow erased itself when he stuck it off the page where it didn't belong," said Mr. Bunn.

"You mean the cartoonist erased it when it went where it didn't belong," chimed in Raggedy.

"Whatever!" shot back Mr. Bunn. "What's important is the arm is no longer here."

"MY ARM! IT'S GONE!" Superbear was now in shock. The very thing he was afraid of losing he actually lost, and he did it to himself … or, rather, the cartoonist did it … or maybe it was the readers' fault, or maybe … whatever the reason, the twins, Terror and Crazy, actually had nothing to do with it like he feared.

"Looks like you and I have something in common there, pal," Trixie said with an understanding smile.

"I don't want to have something in common with you," Superbear cried. "I want my arm back."

"Well, thanks a lot," Trixie responded. "I love you, too."

"Stinky, you've got to draw me a new arm," Superbear pleaded. "You can do it. I know you can. You draw all the time."

"But I'm not THE cartoonist, Superbear," Stinky replied. "You need to go to him for this."

"Okay Mr. Cartoonist, please draw me a new arm," Superbear asked half-heartedly. "See? He didn't do it. And he's not going to do it. He hasn't drawn Trixie a new arm. Why would he draw me one? Besides, he's the reason why I lost this arm in the first place. It's his story."

"So please can you draw me a new arm?" pleaded Super-bear once again.

"Well, okay," replied Stinky. "I don't know why I'm trying to do this. It's not going to work."

"Hurry!" Superbear pleaded once again. "It hurts."

"How can it hurt?" interjected Raggedy. "You're a stuffed animal."

"I don't care," responded Superbear. "It hurts deep inside."

"Yeah, I think your pride muscle has been bruised," chimed in Trixie. "I've been there … had that ailment, too."

"There," said Stinky. "That's the best I can do."

"You call that an arm?" exclaimed Superbear. "It looks like a deformed cactus. Try it again."

"I can't do any better than that," Stinky protested. "Besides, you moved around too much while I was drawing."

"Here, let me try," said Natalie, erasing Stinky's efforts. "I can't do much worse."

"Okay, but hurry," Stinky squeezed his eyes shut. "This is driving me nuts."

"Hey, I'd like to give you a hand," said Raggedy, "But I need the two I've got … such as they are. I don't even have fingers."

"What do you think?" said Natalie when she finished.

"I don't know," said Superbear. "I've seen better looking tree branches."

"I think we'd better think of something else," commented Mr. Bunn. "This isn't working."

"You know, the readers really do have a part in this," Stinky said while he erased Natalie's efforts. "Maybe they'd like to take a crack at it.

"Okay, but tell them to be gentle," Stinky said. "I'm fragile"

Chapter 10: Draw an Arm … Save a Bear

HELP SAVE SUPERBEAR!

Get out your pencils, kids. Draw the bear a new arm and save him from humiliation.

"Whoa! That tickles," said Superbear. "This reader is pretty good."

"Hey, that's not bad," Superbear exclaimed. "What do you think, Stinky?

"I think that since the cartoonist is probably not going to draw your arm again for much of the rest of this story, it would only be fitting for one of the readers to step forward and take care of that task on every page from here on out."

"So, what do you say, readers?" Stinky asked. "Sharpen your pencil. Wherever you see Superbear without an arm through the rest of this book, go ahead and draw it in."

"And I promise I will be happy with whatever you create," Superbear said.

Chapter 11: Not that Bad ... but Bad

As things turned out, life was not as bad as our characters thought it would be. It was sort of bad, but not real bad ... not as bad as it could have been. But make no mistake about it, it was still bad ... and in some ways, not too bad.

Natalie was able to make room for "Terror" and "Crazy" in her room, and they weren't as "terrorizing" or "crazy" once they understood the rules of the house. Mom was a big help there.

Stinky didn't mind sleeping on the dining room table … too much. "Now I know how a Thanksgiving turkey feels," he thought to himself.

Plus, during the day, the area under the table gave him a nice little hideaway where he could write his cartoon stories.

Aunt Smoochie-kiss was just as annoying as ever with her big smoochie-kisses. Everyone would always cringe a little bit whenever she started a sentence with, "Bless your heart …" because they never knew what was going to come out of her mouth next … but they knew it wasn't going to be good.

"Bless your heart, Natalie," Aunt Smoochie-kiss would say. "Your poor hairbrush would snap in two if you ever tried to run it through that mop you call hair on your head."

"Yes, Aunt Beulah," Natalie would say through clenched teeth.

Yet in spite of her annoyances, Stinky and Natalie and all the stuffed characters would sort of feel sorry for Aunt Smoochie-kiss. She would try to be happy and make everyone laugh with her special balloon creations. She'd blow up these long balloons and twist them around into animals and silly hats. It was funny at first but it quickly grew old because that's all she knew how to do.

But there was also a real sadness that lurked just beneath the surface with Aunt Smoochie-kiss. Most likely she knew she didn't belong in Stinky and Natalie's home, but she probably didn't know what else she was supposed to do. So Stinky and Natalie would wear her stupid balloon creations on their heads around the house because they wanted to keep Aunt Smoochie-kiss happy.

Chapter 12: Taking Care of the Critters

As for the stuffed animals, Natalie never let them out of her sight because of Terror and Crazy. She would cram them into her backpack and take them to school with her … which was often a pretty funny sight.

Occasionally Natalie had too many books to carry in her backpack. So to help her out, Stinky would take Super-bear to school with him. Stinky did whatever he could to keep him hidden. It would be disastrous if any of his friends found him carrying a stuffed animal to school.

What he didn't count on was one of his enemies finding out. Just as Stinky was reaching into his backpack for his after school snack money one day, who should show up but his favorite bully ... Biff.

"Awww … isn't that cute?" Biff asked, reaching into Stinky's book bag. "Are we feeling a bit insecure these days that we have to bring our widdle teddy bear to school with us?"

"Hey, Biff, give me that back," said Stinky reaching for Superbear. "That's not mine. I'm holding it for my sister."

"Oh, you're holding it for your sister, huh?" Biff replied. "Does your sister know this is really a 'superbear' and 'superbears' have 'super powers' ..."

"… like flying?" And with that Biff hurled Superbear with all his might into a wall of lockers. The impact made such a loud noise that everyone in the hallway noticed Stinky retrieving his stuffed animal and putting him back into his book bag.

"Look!" someone said. "Stinky Stevens carries a stuffed animal to school with him."

"Sorry about that, Superbear," Stinky said, obviously unaware of the crowd around him. "I'll try to do a better job of keeping you hidden."

"Look!" someone else said, "Stinky Stevens talks to the stuffed animal he carries to school with him."

"He's so weird," another person said. "Their whole family is weird."

Stinky was certainly aware of THAT comment. It was like a knife going into his heart. More than anything he wanted people to see him as just another normal kid at school. But he was "cursed" with knowing the truth about the world around them ... that is, everyone is a cartoon character drawn by a wonderful, loving cartoonist.

And having a relative like Aunt Smoochie-kiss didn't help matters any. "I just hope she doesn't show her face around school any time soon," Stinky thought to himself. "I'd be ruined for life."

Now you know when a cartoon character makes a comment like that, what do you think the cartoonist is going to do? The possibilities are just too irresistible.

Chapter 13: Oh No! It Can't Be!

Just then, Stinky heard a ruckus from down at the end of the hall. There was a crowd. There was laughter. There was Aunt Smoochie-kiss. And there was Stinky's heart, sinking down into the pit of his stomach.

There she was in all her glory. Aunt Smoochie-kiss was giving out smoochie kisses, blowing up balloons, and singing out, "bless your pea pickin' heart" to everyone she met.

Standing next to her was Natalie, with one of Aunt Smoochie-kiss's balloon creations on her head, looking like she wanted to go crawl into a hole.

Natalie caught sight of Stinky. "Oh, Stinky, you've got to do something," she pleaded. "Aunt Smoochie-kiss came to pick us up from school and she's making me look stupid in front of all my friends."

"I … I don't know WHAT to do," Stinky responded.

Meanwhile Aunt Smoochie-kiss was having all kinds of fun laughing with the kids and passing out her balloon creations ... not realizing they were really laughing AT her.

Then somebody from the back of the crowd said to his friends, "Hey, everybody, come look at the clown! We've got a clown at school today!"

"Where?" Aunt Smoochie-kiss responded. "I love clowns. Where's the clown?"

This made the crowd of students roar with laughter even more. In looking around Aunt Smoochie-kiss suddenly noticed her own reflection in a classroom window and it stopped her in her tracks. She couldn't move. She looked at her big floppy hat, and her striped tights, and her funny looking dress in a way she hadn't seen before. She was stunned. For a moment, Stinky and Natalie thought she was going to cry. They had never seen a grownup cry before and they weren't sure what they were going to do if she did.

"Hey, clown," someone from the crowd shouted. "Gimme one of those balloon hat things you make."

"I want one too," said another.

"You'll have to excuse me for a moment," Aunt Smoochie-kiss said, and she dashed off into the little girls room.

Stinky and Natalie just stood there looking at each other, not sure what they were supposed to do.

"Do you think I should go in after her?" Natalie asked.

Before Stinky had a chance to reply, out came Aunt Smoochie-kiss with bright red lips and bright red circles on her cheeks from her lipstick, and she had a bright blue bottle cap stuck to the tip of her nose with a piece of chewing gum.

"Gather around, everyone!" Aunt Smoochie-kiss shouted. "I've got a smoochie kiss and a balloon hat for everyone!"

And Aunt Smoochie-kiss spent the next hour keeping the kids entertained while they waited for their rides home from school.

Later that week, Stinky, Natalie, and the stuffed animals were still trying to figure out what all had happened.

"I don't know what went on awhile back, but Aunt Smoochie-kiss sure seems a lot happier these days," commented Natalie.

"Yeah, I'm even starting to really enjoy having her around," added Stinky.

"And have you noticed?" chimed in Superbear, "She hasn't use the phrase 'Bless your heart' once since she picked us up from school that day."

Chapter 14: Just Clowning Around

Then all the stuffed animals went limp as Mom came into the room. "Hey, kids, I've got some news for you. Aunt Beulah and her grandkids are leaving."

"Leaving?" Stinky and Natalie both responded. "We were just getting used to having her around."

"Aunt Beulah has decided to go to clown school, and it's in the same town as her daughter," Mom said. "Things have improved in her home so Aunt Beulah is going to move in with her. Trevor and Tracy will be back with their parents. Isn't that wonderful?"

"I don't know what to say," Stinky replied.

"Come say goodbye," Mom continued. "They're leaving this afternoon."

Aunt Smoochie-kiss greeted them with one of her patented smoochie kisses and said, "You kids have been wonderful to my grandbabies and me when I needed a helping hand."

"Here's something for you to help remember me," she continued.

"What is it?" asked Natalie. "Another balloon animal?"

"Nope," Aunt Smoochie-kiss responded. "It's a drawing I did."

"I didn't know you could draw, Aunt Beulah," Stinky said.

"There are a lot of things you didn't know I could do," she replied. "In fact, I didn't know I could do them either."

"This is a drawing of an arm with a hand on it," said Natalie.

"That's to remind you of the helping hand you gave me," Aunt Smoochie-kiss replied. "I'm going to be a clown. What do you think of this name? ... 'Aunt Smoochie-kiss,' because of all the smoochie kisses I give."

"I think it fits," said Stinky. "It's as if you've been called that all along."

With that, Aunt Smoochie-kiss gave them all another big smoochie-kiss, strapped her grandbabies into the back seat of her car, and drove off.

Back in her room, Natalie held up Aunt Smoochie-kiss's drawing. "What am I going to do with this?" she said.

Stinky had a thought. "Stand up in front of this drawing, Superbear," he said. "You don't suppose this will work as a replacement for your arm, do you?"

"Huh? It's worth a shot, I guess," Superbear replied.

Once he got the drawing lined up with his arm, Stinky pulled away the paper and the drawing stayed attached to Superbear's body.

"It works! It works!" Superbear screamed. "I knew the cartoonist would heal me. I knew it. I never doubted him at all. It's just a matter of having enough faith. The cartoonist loves me after all."

"Oh, is that right?" a very one-armed Trixie said with a bit of disdain.

"The cartoonist ... he. ..." Superbear stammered. "Oh, I'm sorry, Trixie ... I don't know WHY he replaced my arm and not yours."

"That's okay, Superbear," Trixie replied. "I'm happy for you. Some day my turn may come." And she gave Superbear her best one-armed hug.

"Well this opens up all kinds of theological possibilities," Raggedy joined in.

"Don't start, Raggedy!" snapped Mr. Bunn.

"But did Aunt Smoochie-kiss really draw the arm? Or did the cartoonist really draw it while making it look like she drew it? And why did Superbear's arm get drawn and not Trixie's? She's waited longer. Did Superbear really have more faith? Or was she just not humble enough?"

"GIVE IT A REST, RAGGEDY!" shouted Mr. Bunn.

And the discussion, such as it was, continued long into the night.

Visit CartoonWorks.com
for more FUN STUFF to see and do!

• Read an award winning Stinky Stevens comic strip and find the latest Stinky Stevens books and products,

• Play fun online jigsaw puzzles and cool games,

• Read hundreds of online comic strips,

• Download dozens of coloring books,

• Download humorous gospel cartoon tracts,

• Plus, childrens books, T-shirts, greeting cards, mugs, caps, stickers, and much, much more,

• ... and learn more about the cartoonist who created it all!

CPSIA information can be obtained at www.ICGtesting.com
Printed in the USA
LVOW091729260712

291700LV00013B/22/P

9 780982 937778